Gay Romance Erotica

Coming Together

Amy Redek

About the Publisher

4Fun Publishing, a member of **BLVNP Incorporated,** 340 S. Lemon #6200, Walnut CA 91789, info@blvnp.com / legal@blvnp.com

NOTE: Due to the highly emotional reaction of some people to works of erotic fiction, any email sent to the above address that contains foul language or religious references is automatically deleted by our anti-spam software and will not be seen. All other communications are welcome.

DISCLAIMER

Please don't be stupid and kill yourself. This book is a work of FICTION. Do not try any new sexual practice that you find in this book. It is fiction and not to be confused with reality. Neither the author nor the publisher or its associates assume any responsibility for any loss, injury, death or legal consequences resulting from acting on the contents in this book. Every character in this book is over 18 years of age. The author's opinions are not to be construed as the opinions of the publisher. The material in this book is for entertainment purposes ONLY. Enjoy.

Coming Together
Gay Romance Erotica

By: Amy Redek

© **Amy Redek 2014**
ISBN: 978-1-62761-869-4

I ALWAYS thought that I would fall in love sometime in the future but never in a hundred years would I have believed that it would be with be with another man. When at school with the boys, dog-eared books would be passed around showing women, at the beginning, being fully clothed and as you turned the pages, the clothing became scantier with every page until you finally got to those that showed them naked.

I didn't realise at the time why they didn't turn me on. I would see the girls in our class and couldn't stand the way that they would look at you and start giggling and couldn't relate them to the pictures I had seen in the books that had been passed round. They were all flat chested and wore hideous clothing which is maybe what turned me off of them.

It was the same in college. At least there, the girls wore decent looking clothes and filled out the blouse or T shirt that they wore. But again, there wasn't anything special about them that would draw my attention to them. I would even have them smile at me on occasions especially when I was a member of our swimming team.

I must admit that I looked strong and healthy, having loved swimming for years prior to joining the team and so had strong looking arms and chest as well as solid thighs. I never dreamed at the time that what they looked at most was what was hidden inside my swimming costume when I left the pool to return to the changing room.

I would look into one of the mirrors above a wash basin to see what they could see. My face was straight as was my nose. My hair was a cross between being light brown and blonde and my eyebrows were straight and the eye lashes a normal size. My eyes were of a light to dark blue and my smile was okay and it showed that my teeth were good and white. I would even flex my muscles to see that didn't have any effect on me, never giving a thought that they were probably looking much lower down my body at the time.

When we had a college ball, I would spend most of my time with the other boys and wouldn't accept any offers to dance with the girls that asked me to dance with them. I would then often get strange looks from the other guys but nothing was said as to what they were thinking, but I know better now. It was later in reflection that I came to realise that they assumed with me not talking about or going out with any of the girls that I was gay. This thought never came into my mind.

I did well enough at the college to be among the top five and to get an offer to be sent off to a university to expand my knowledge on ancient history, me having come out top of the class on the subject. I had always loved reading books of the period which helped in my achievement at the college.

So off to our local university I went and it was there that I fell in love. It was there that I met Alex who was studying the same as me, and it began with us comparing notes as to what we did or didn't know in the sphere of the ancients. I was following Alexander while he was learning more of Hannibal. Maybe it was because of Alexander being gay that attracted me to his life and connections to others of the same ilk. It was never known if Hannibal was gay or not, but with the men of both armies being away from home for months and years at a time, many of them had sex together without there being any women in their armies to satisfy their need for sex.

It didn't take long for both of us to find out we were both semi historians and so would spend time together to discuss what we each were aiming at. We had different rooms allocated to us but with a little persuasion, Alex got his roommate to swap over with me. So in the evenings after lights out in bed, we could still continue with the pros and cons of each other's subject.

We had our likes and dislikes and compromised to both enjoy being with each other. The major difference between us was that I was a swimmer, which he wasn't, and he was a ski fan, which led us on to want to teach each other of the two differences in our sporting activities. There wasn't any snow near the university but it had a swimming pool, so it was me first to show and teach him how to swim.

It was a twenty-five-metre long pool and had a small trough round on the inside to take the overflow of water that was being constantly pumped out into the pool to keep it fresh. This was ideal for him, when we were in the pool at the shallow end for him to grip this trough and stretch himself out for me to hold him so that he could follow my instructions on how to use his legs. It was also to increase the muscles there, which was much needed in swimming.

It was a good job that my waist was below the water level, for with my left hand under his chest to keep his front end up, my right hand was up under his groin so that he could thrash his legs. The problem for me was that with my right hand where it was, I could feel his penis that was inside his costume and for some inexplicable reason, my own penis would become enlarged to then be a rampant cock.

Fortunately, it would shrink back to its normal size by the time it came for us to leave the pool to have a shower to wash off traces of the chlorine from the pool. As we would have this shower together, I noted that his penis was about the same size as mine with them both being deflated.

This would happen to me every time I held him in the water until the time came for him to be taught how to use his hands to help propel him through the water and of the way to turn his head to take in some air when actually swimming on his own.

I could still remember the way I felt when I used to have my hand up at his groin, feeling his penis and having mine become erect when we were in our beds at night, and so would jerk myself off into some tissues when I knew he was asleep.

Semester time came round and it was just at the beginning of this that an event happened that changed our lives. With us being free from the university, it was now time for him to show me how to ski, and so off we went into the mountains where there was packed snow that a lot of people used for their skiing.

It was on the third day that, as he went down the slope, one of the clips on his boot parted and sent him off at an angle towards some trees. The collision was inevitable and he had his hands out to try to fend himself off from a full body crash. But in having his arms out at full stretch to do this, he broke both arms and finished up sliding down the slope on his back.

It took me a little while to get to where was then being seen to by some people who had seen this accident and an ambulance had been called for. It wasn't long before he was on a stretcher and I went along with him in the ambulance that was taking him to the local hospital. It was fortunate that he hadn't broken the collar bones but each arm had two breaks and so they were put into plaster with his arms then bent across his chest.

He was inside for three days to make sure that he was okay to be discharged, but then lay the problem of his eating and seeing to his ablutions, which he was incapable of to see to himself with his arms in plaster. With him now being a very close friend of mine, immediately volunteered to help him and got a grateful grin for the offer. It was fortunate that his parents, who lived on the other side of the country, have been available to rent him a small bedsit so that he didn't have to traipse back and forth during holidays. This had been done before he'd even entered the university, and so it was to this bedsit that we had a car drive us to.

Alex kept apologising for ruining our semester and thanking me for offering to be his nurse and cook, to wash and feed him. On arrival at his rented bedsit, I found that it lived up to its name, for there was only one bed for sleeping. The battered sofa in the small living room had to be small to have gotten it inside, it only being a two-seater and less than five feet long.

'The bed's big enough for the two of us if you don't mind sleeping with me,' Alex said as I surveyed this abode which only took a few minutes. 'Also helping me with the problem I've now got.'

'What's that?' I asked.

'I'm busting for a piss,' and so I followed him into the small, very small bathroom for him to stand in front of the pan where I pulled down the zipper of his trouser front and pulled out his cock which I held to direct his stream of piss into the pan. Because of the confined space of this bathroom, I had to stand behind him so as to keep him balanced. With my left hand round his waist and my right hand holding his cock, the front of my body was pressed up against his rear end. What with me holding his cock in my hand and feeling him pissing, my own cock grew inside of my trousers and I'm sure he felt it but he didn't make any comment about it when he'd finished and I shook his cock, almost rubbing it to make sure that it was empty before putting it back inside his trousers.

With that done, we went back into the small living room and got him to sit down while I made some coffee for us. While waiting for the water to boil, I checked the bedroom and was pleased to see that the bed was the biggest piece of furniture in the whole place and it would sleep two without being cramped.

I had to hold his cup as he drank his coffee and when both cups were empty, told him that the fridge was empty and that I had to go out to get some food. He couldn't stop apologising for putting me through all of this knowing that I also had to feed him too. I kept waving this off and with making sure he was settled, went out and was away for a good hour before I returned with enough food for a few days plus a take away so that we could at least eat something straight away. I had bought a concoction of food that I could feed to him piece by piece and wondered if this was what is known as being piecemeal. Food for thought. Ha ha!

With having had his shirt taken off for the hospital to plaster his arms, he only had had his heavy coat wrapped round his shoulders, so I covered his top half with a blanket until it was time for bed. Before that, it was into the bathroom again for me to brush his teeth and with there only being the one brush, had to use it myself to do mine. Then it was to the toilet pan where I again pulled his cock out to guide the stream of piss into the pan with me getting another erection by having my body close up to his.

Then it was into the bedroom where, as he was standing up, opened and pulled down his trousers and underpants and had him then sit on the bed while I took these off his legs after having taken off his shoes and socks. In doing this, I was down on my knees with his semi hard cock just a few inches away from my face and had a sudden urge to want to take it into my mouth, but refrained as I didn't want to upset our relationship in doing so. But the urge was there and it didn't go away even getting him settled in the bed and I know that he saw that I had an erection when I was fully undressed and got into bed beside him.

I had turned out the lamp and we lay there in the dark for quite some time before he spoke.

'Darren,' he began, that being my name. 'I can't thank you enough for what you are doing.'

'Hush,' I said, rolling over onto my side, seeing his face in the gloom of the room, and couldn't help that my cock was now pressed up against his thigh. 'You're my….friend, and what are friends for?'

'Well, as a friend,' he said, 'I couldn't help seeing and feeling that you've got a hard on, so why don't you jerk yourself off. There's some tissues on the side of you.'

'You don't mind me doing it?'I asked.

'Well, you do it often enough in our room at the uni,' he said.

As my cock was really beginning to hurt me with it being so hard, wanted to do just that, but was going to wait until he was asleep. So now with having him already knowing that I jerked off, rolled back and got some tissues and with my cock in my hand, moved the flesh up and down over the solid flesh beneath it and gave myself up to the pleasure in doing just that. I couldn't help the groan that I gave as my cum filled the tissues that I held in my other hand until I'd finished and wiped the head clean before dropping the tissues out of the bed.

'Was that good?' he asked as I settled back down.

'I needed that,' I told him.

'Er, Darren? Would…would you do the same for me as I can't do it myself for my cock is hurting me bad,' he said. There had been a tremor in his voice as he asked me of that, and felt that I couldn't deny him to have the same release that I had just had. Also, it was what I wanted to do and had been afraid that by me asking to do it to him could have split us apart.

So I rolled back over to get some more tissues and with them in my left hand, rolled back onto my other side and took hold of his hard cock that was lying up on his stomach.

I could feel his heart beat pulsating away inside the blood that kept his cock up and hard and I revelled in the fact that I was doing what I had yearned to do for months now. I found that I was drooling at the mouth as my hand moved up and down the solid bar of meat, keeping a firm grip as I jerked him off, hearing him give out a big sigh with me doing it for him. So the pleasure wasn't all mine as I kept onto seeing to him until I felt his leg that I was leaning against began to tremble and quickly got the tissues over the head of his cock just in time to catch the cum that erupted out of the eye of his cock.

I wondered then as I kept squeezing his cock to get the last remnants of his cum out of his cock, what it would taste like. I felt the strength of his cock lessen slightly and knew that he had finished so released him and rolled back and dropped the tissue onto the floor, knowing that I could put them down the toilet pan in the morning.

'Thank you, Darren, for seeing to me when I can't myself,' he said in a low soft voice. 'I've been wanting you to do that for me for some time now for I know that I'm in love with you. If I could move, I would show you by kissing you. Do you have any love for me? Enough to kiss me?'

'Alex. I've been wanting to do that from the first time of feeling you in the swimming pool and I love you too,' I said as I rolled over to him, and keeping my body away from his plastered arm, leaned in and kissed him. It lasted for several minutes with him kissing me back. Our soft lips mashing against each other and having our tongues touch between our open mouths.

'That was nice,' he said when I rolled back on the bed. 'I've been wanting to do that to you, too,' he said. 'I even wanted to have your cock in my hand and also to take the head into my mouth to suck on and have you cum for me to taste before swallowing.'

'I, too, feel the same. I was tempted when you were sitting on the edge of the bed as I took your clothes off. With it being so close to me I wanted to take you into my mouth for the same reason,' I said.

'Well, I don't have to use my hands to do that,' he said,' but you can help me tomorrow to do what I've wanted to do for ages now.'

'I'll do the same for you in the morning and we won't even have to get out of bed for me to do it,' I told him.

'Oh, if only I could do it now,' he sighed. 'Are we now lovers?' he asked.

'I can't think of anything better,' I replied, stroking his thigh, the back of my hand rubbing his flaccid cock, knowing that it would be up nice and hard in the morning for me to show just how much I loved him. I kept stroking his thigh until I fell asleep.

I WOKE up a bit disorientated for a few seconds wondering where the hell I was, but on feeling the leg of Alex against one of mine, came to realise where, and why I was there in bed with him. Dawn had broken and we had light in the small bedroom and turning my head, saw that Alex was still asleep. Then I remembered as to how I was going to wake him up.

I slowly eased myself down under the bed covers until I could see, very faintly, that he had an erection and it was lying up on his stomach. Mind you, I had one too, but I wanted to show the love I had for him so I gently lifted his cock upright and licked my lips before leaning over him and taking the head of his rampant cock into my mouth.

My heart beat increased and my mind went wild at now having what I nearly did yesterday when I undressed him. It was hard in my hand but soft in my mouth as I eased the foreskin down with my lips, loving all the sensations that flew round in my body as I began to suck and run my tongue over the bare flesh that I had uncovered.

I felt his leg move under me and heard him give out a groan as I teased the head of his cock, running my tongue over the G-string that was an erotic part of the body. With him coming awake, I now began to move my hand up and down, moving the soft skin that seemed to glide over the solid flesh that it covered. It was in a firm grip as I was slowly jerking him off and sucking and licking his cock at the same time.

I now knew that I had found my forte and the reason why females had never attracted me for it was what I had in my mouth that I wanted. I was in heaven, as I sucked and rubbed his cock, waiting for him to cum in my mouth for me to find out if this was what I had been longing for quite some time and not having realised it.

It wasn't long before I felt his thigh muscles tighten up and his hips beginning to move as the head swelled a little more and have the first salvo of his cum gush out of the eye of his cock to hit the back of my throat. It was about six pulsating throbs of his cock that I felt as more of his cum that never seemed to end, filling my mouth so much so that I had to swallow what I had there to be able to take in the rest that he was giving me.

I felt his body relax with another groan from him and with him being empty was now able to lick the last remnants of his cum from around the head of his lovely throbbing cock, to find that his cum was almost tasteless. The hardness now seemed to be leaving his erection as it felt soft in my hand and so with a final suck and lick on the head, lifted my head back up off of him and let his still fairly hard cock flop back onto his stomach.

I moved up the bed till my head came clear of the covers to see that he had a big smile on his face.

'That was lovely, Darren,' he said. 'Can I kiss you for that lovely way of being woken up?' I kept moving up until I was able to lean over him without pressing myself against the plastered arm that was across his chest. Our lips met as we kissed and even had his tongue enter my mouth to play with mine as we kissed. 'That's the first time that anyone has ever done that to me,' he said after we had broken off the kissing of each other.

'The first time for me to do such a thing,' I told him. 'Now I know why I didn't have time for any female. It was what you have that I needed to fulfill my life.'

'I can feel that you've got a hard on, so help me out of bed so that I can give you the same pleasure that you have just given me,' he said. I had no objection to that for my cock was really throbbing now and so got out of my side of the bed and went round to his side and pulled the covers down, noticing that his cock had almost deflated now. I eased his legs towards me as he struggled to turn his body round at the same time for me to then pull him towards me so that his legs came off the bed and got his feet down onto the carpet.

He was still lying on his back and so pulled him upright and helped him stand up on his own two feet. It was almost funny to see him standing there naked with his plastered arms across his chest, and he moved back a little from the bed. 'Sit down on the bed,' he said, 'with your legs open and help me kneel down without falling on top of you.'

This I did, holding his shoulders to help ease him down onto his knees between my legs. His plastered arms came onto my thighs as he then leaned forward. 'You'll have to help me in this,' he said, 'for I can't pull your lovely looking cock forward, nor will I be able to hold it.'

So I lifted my cock up and bent it towards his open mouth that came down upon the head and felt the heat of his mouth as his lips closed round the base of the head and felt his tongue begin to move over the flesh that was bared for him to also suck on.

I put one hand against his bobbing head as he sucked on me and with the other hand, rubbed my cock up and down in time with his head movements, as though it has him doing this to me. Such was my need for release, I was feeling my cum starting to move and released my cock and held his head and gently began to push my cock upwards to his own downward movement, taking it easy so that I wouldn't choke him as I technically face fucked him.

He gave a cough as the first emission hit the back of his throat and then had his lips clamp themselves firmly round my cock as he took in the rest of my cum until his mouth was full and my cock empty. I felt my cum being moved round in his mouth before feeling the suction as he then swallowed it. He finished off by licking the head clean of any residue of my cum before lifting his head up to release me though giving the bared flesh a final kiss. He looked up at me with his eyes sparkling and a big grin on his face.

'That's the first time I've done that, and it…it was just great, and wished that we had started doing this earlier,' he said. 'Help me up please.' So I managed to get my hands up under his arm pits and lifted him up as I stood up until we were both on our feet. He leaned in and kissed me again. 'But now comes the nasty bit for you, for I need a crap and you'll have to wipe my ass.' I gave him a grimace but with a smile that made him laugh, the first since the accident.

So it was into the bathroom we went and then found how difficult it was in that confined space to be able to wipe his ass after he had finished, but we managed it with me then using a wet flannel to really make sure that his ass was clean. I then got him to the wash basin to wash his face and brush his teeth before seeing to my own ablutions before washing myself etc.

As small as his bedsit was, at least it was quite warm inside and so we stayed naked and got him to sit down at the small dining table while I got him a bowl of cereals in milk and fed him a spoonful at a time. It was just like feeding a baby and wiping the dribbling milk from his chin. I also cut up the toast into small pieces to feed him one bit at a time and also had to hold the coffee cup up to his lips to drink. All that had to be done before I could have my breakfast.

THAT WAS our pattern for the next five weeks and it was the week before we were due back at the university, that I took him to the hospital where he was x-rayed and they were pleased to see that the bones had mended and so had the plastered arms released for them to check properly though with the advice to take it easy in all that he did. Not to lift anything heavy, to which he gave a smirk as he had looked down at my groin at what was said, plus a few other things he was not to do.

It had been difficult to dress him before we had gone to the hospital, the first time since being at the bedsit, but now he should be able to do it himself now, was my thought. It wasn't until we were back there that it was then the first time that he was able to put his arms round and hug me, giving me many kisses, saying that I deserved more for having taken so much trouble in looking after him whilst in plaster. Though after that first day after having to sit down on the toilet, he was then able to have a piss that way by staying naked, so I didn't have to hold his cock any more for that little job, much to my regret, though I didn't tell him of this.

It took him the whole of that week to get used to now being able to move his arms and do what he wanted to get his strength back before us returning to the university.

There, back in our own room again, we would, nearly every night, sleep together in one of the beds and also having oral sex, though it was during our second week that we went further in making love to each other by introducing anal sex between us.

It was Alex who wanted to start and be the first and as I had already run this through my mind, agreed for I wanted to feel him inside me too, just as he had said of me. During a break, he'd gone into town and bought a bag of condoms and so that night, we began in further cementing our relationship.

'I've been wanting for us to do this ever since our first night in bed together, Darren,' he said when we were naked in our room. 'To have you inside of me instead of just the mouth.' I took him into my arms and kissed him.

'Are you sure that you want us to do this?' I asked.

'Darren. Ever since we began my swimming lessons and you had your hand under me, I fell in love with you then. I looked at what you had when in the shower and I wanted to take hold of you and do what we now do together,' he said still holding me. Shades of heaven. He was saying almost the way I had felt then. He carried on.

'Then with my arms in plaster, you were like a mother to me and with that first night in bed, feeling your hardness up against my thigh, I wanted there and then to kiss what I felt. Not only kiss it, but have it in my mouth to suck and show you just how much I had fallen in love with you.'

'You are saying nearly all that was in my mind too when I was with you. In the pool, in the shower and also watching you getting into bed. I too wanted to take you into my mouth when I first undressed you and had you sitting down on the edge of the bed with what I wanted right in front of my eyes. It was when I woke up in the morning and you were

still asleep that I took a chance to show you how much I loved you…..'
He interrupted me.

'And I loved you doing it and knew that you loved me as much as I loved you and now I want what I've sucked and played with for weeks now, inside of me. To feel you cumming inside me and I want you to really know how much I love you by having you fuck me.'

'It's what I've wanted to do, Alex, and then to have you fuck me which will say how much I love you too,' and we kissed each other, having and feeling our erections clash and get pressed together between our bodies. As we both wanted the same, we soon broke apart and Alex went down onto his knees and gave my erection a few sucks before he rolled a condom down over the head and shaft of my cock.

He had also bought a pot of cream that he then opened and dipped his finger inside and coated the head of the condom and I saw that he put some cream to his backside before getting onto his bed, to be on his knees, me seeing where he had put that other blob of cream.

My cock was really throbbing now at seeing where I was going to put it and got onto his bed and moved in between his open legs. Had nature intended this for us, for the entrance to his ass was at the same level as my throbbing cock and didn't need my hand to guide it to the blob of cream as I put my hands onto his hips and moved closer to him until the head of my covered cock was touching the cream that covered the entrance to his ass.

I felt his body tremble when he felt me touching him there and gave out a little cry as he felt the head of my cock expanding his ring piece. I nearly stopped, thinking that I was really hurting him, but the head slipped in and I was able to push even further inside his ass until my thighs were tight up to the cheeks of his bum. I could feel the muscle that was there, flexing itself round my shaft and I was thrilled at me now having my cock up inside the man that I loved.

He had given out a gasp and a low groan when I was then fully in there. 'Oh, Darren. I can really feel it throbbing and I'm getting some wonderful shivers running up and down my spine with you now inside me,' he said in a shaky voice.

'And I love being where I am now, feeling the inside heat of you and having that muscle squeezing me,' I said.

'Well, start moving and really fuck me,' he grunted, and so I began moving myself back and forth, having my cock sliding along in his back passage, getting a wonderful thrill of being where I now was.

'I love... this... Darren,' he panted as I ploughed this virgin meadow, having the pressure of his insides all the way round my cock as it moved inside him. But the pleasure was short lived for I could feel my cum start to move up my cock and I held his hips tighter as I then began to have my cum shooting out into the condom.

'Oh, Darren. I love this,' he gasped as I came to a stop, leaning over his rear end as I felt almost exhausted in having fucked and given him my cum that had needed the release from my aching balls. 'I can feel it still throbbing and exciting all the nerves of my body.'

I straightened myself up and began to pull out of him to his cry and sat back on my heels, thinking of the pleasure I'd just had in my fucking of him. He was quick to turn round and without bothering about tissues, pulled the condom off my cock and took the head into his mouth to suck and lick the head that still had some of my cum coating it. He was actually gurgling as he sucked and rubbed my still hard cock and I stroked the hair of his head as it bobbed on my cock. This fucking of him could only have lasted about four minutes but it had been such a pleasure that I wished that it could have lasted longer.

With him having licked the head clean, rose up and hugged me, kissing me at the same time.

'I can't wait to give you the same pleasure that you have just given me,' he said between his feverish kissing of my lips, me getting some of my own cum smeared on my lips which I licked off when we broke apart. 'My turn now,' he said and moved and got a fresh condom and gave it to me after he'd unwrapped it. I had to lay down to give the head of his cock a few sucks before rising back up to roll the rubber down over his hard and pulsating member.

He had also picked up the pot of cream and saw him smear some over the head of his covered cock as I went onto my knees and felt him put some cream to the entry of my ass, quivering at the coldness of the cream being put there. My heart was pumping away in my chest wondering if it was going to be painful with him widening my asshole. But whatever, I was going to endure it because I loved Alex and was going to let him have the same pleasure that I had when I fucked him.

Even so, my body trembled when I felt the head of his cock move into the cream and then touch the entrance to my ass. His hands now moved onto my hips and I felt the pressure as the head of his cock began to move so as to widen the hole that his cock was now about to enter. The pain was increasing as the muscle which I couldn't control, wouldn't relax and was about to cry out for him to stop when all of a sudden, his cock entered my ass and slid right in until I had his thighs tight up to the cheeks of my bum.

Wow! The pain had suddenly lessened and I could feel his cock throbbing away as all kinds of tingles ran mad throughout my body, the sensations making me gasp. These increased as he then moved his cock back and forth inside me, thrilling me with all the different feelings running round in my body.

The entry pain was now forgotten as he moved inside me, his hands holding my hips tight as he slid about, annoying my prostate gland that was nothing to the thrill I was getting as he fucked me. If this was love, may it last forever, were my thoughts, but it didn't, for it wasn't long before he was really reaming my backside, his fingers digging into my hips as he pulled me back onto his forward thrusting of himself into me.

I then remembered my Shakespeare from Twelfth Night, "if music be the food of love, play on". But for me it was, if fucking my ass be the food of love, keep going.

I had felt his cockhead expanding and knew that he was letting loose his cum to fill the condom and had him come to a stop, leaning over me as his cock kept on throbbing away inside my ass. My muscle was there, flexing itself away like mad and became even more so as Alex began to pull out of me. I even tried with my muscle to hold him inside me, but failed and had him slip out. I could hear his heavy breathing and quickly turned round to pay homage to the totem that I would now worship.

He was sitting back on his heels as I had done, panting away, and also didn't bother with tissues to pull the condom off of his still up and hard cock and took the head into mouth to suck any of his cum that might still be inside as well as licking what still was left on the head. I think I was slobbering as I tried to get as much of his cock into my mouth as I'd just had up in my ass. But I eventually released him and straightened up and went into his arms for us to kiss.

THIS THEN became a regular means of making love every other night while at the university, that other night would be us laying top to toe to suck on each other at the same time in what is known as a sixty-niner. It soon became apparent that we were gay, for we were never apart and at odd times could be seen holding hands. We never went to any of the dances that were held and only mixed with a few of the other students there, noting that there were others the same as us.

Afterword

Darren and Alex stayed their three years at the university and because of the fifty-page thesis that Darren wrote, was rated as being the top student and was awarded a doctorate and offered the job there to teach Ancient history. He only accepted this when it was agreed that Alex would be able to teach with him, and so they settled in there and taught new students during the day and made love to each other at night.

THE END

Here is a sample from another story you may enjoy:

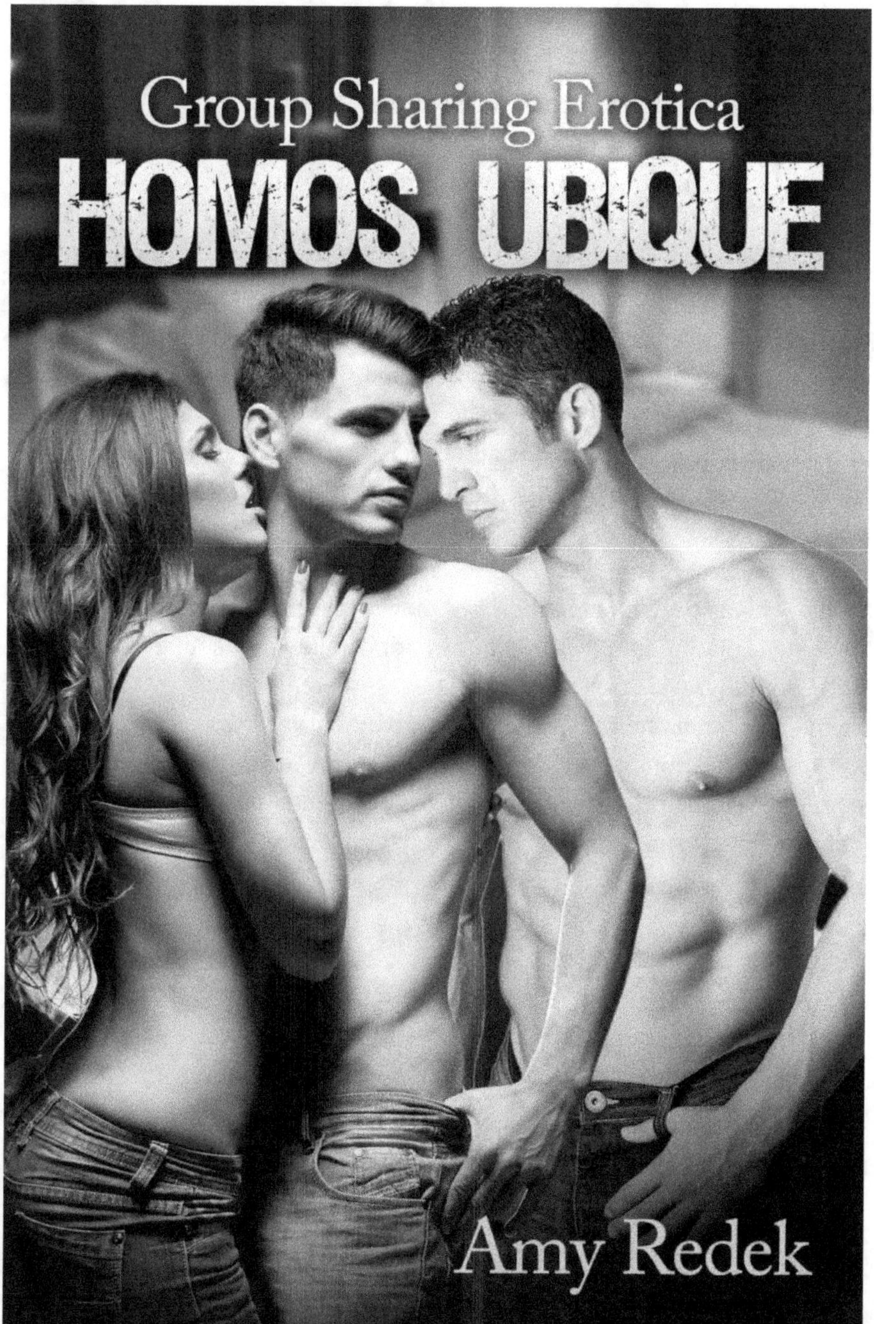
Group Sharing Erotica
HOMOS UBIQUE
Amy Redek

WHEN I was courting and finally married Cyndi, I didn't know that she was bi-sexual. In fact it was two years after our marriage that I found out by accident. That was because I arrived home earlier than normal as we'd had a problem at work and they closed down early, the reason's not relevant, but what I found at home was.

I'd parked the car in the garage and went in via the back door which wasn't locked and expected to find Cyndi in the lounge, but was wrong, and wondered where she was. I knew she was in the house because of the back door not being locked, and so I assumed she was in the bathroom. Wrong again, for she was in the bedroom. That was then a shock for me, for she was not alone, for there was Vera on the bed with her. What was more, was that both of them were naked and Cyndi was between the legs of Vera sucking and licking at her pussy.

I was transfixed at the sight, never having dreamt that Cyndi was bi-sexual, plating another woman. I hadn't made any sound opening the door so they were unaware that I was there, hearing the sounds of Cyndi's sucking and the moans being given out by Vera, squirming about at the ministrations that she was getting, her eyes closed and her hands pounding the bed as I guessed by her movements that she was just about to have an orgasm.

I saw her body writhe on the bed and then relax at having had her release before she opened her eyes.

'Christ!' she exclaimed, her legs closing against Cyndi's head, making her squirm and bring her hands up to prise the legs open for her to breathe and speak.

'What the hell you doing?' Cyndi asked, looking up at the wide eyes of Vera.

'It's him!' she cried, her face now a bright red in having been caught in the act. 'Your husband!' pointing at me in the doorway.

'Oh shit!' Cyndi said, turning her head for me to see her eyes wide open as well now, her face going red and saw that her lips and mouth were wet from the juices of Vera. 'What are you doing coming home so early?' she asked, moving out from between Vera's legs that closed up and her rolling over onto her stomach, burying her face into the pillow.

'More to the point,' I said, looking at her naked body as she turned and sat up, 'is what the hell do you think you were doing?'

'Having sex, you prat! What else did it look like?' was her retort.

'Why?' I asked and then realised that it was a stupid question.

'Don't tell him,' came the muffled voice of Vera from the pillow.

'Why not?' Cyndi replied, half turning her body and giving the cute bum cheeks a stroke before turning back to me. 'It's because we like it. We've been having sex together ever since school.'

'But you're now married....to me!' I cried.

'So? I like having sex with you as I also like having sex with Vera,' she replied.

'But two women doing it together. It's.....it's not right,' I exclaimed.

'Men do it together as well as women,' she came back at me. 'Maybe you should do it and then everything would be alright. Why not try Bruce? He's gay and I'm sure he liked to have it with you.'

Bruce was a friend of ours, both of us having known him for years and quite often came round to our house for a drink and a chat. So with her saying that he was gay was news to me for I hadn't guessed, even though he was single. Little did I know what was running through her mind at this point but I found out a few days later.

'Now get out of here and let Vera get dressed,' she said, getting up from the foot of the bed and pushing me out of the bedroom. With her then closing the door, I went downstairs and poured myself out a drink, musing over what she had said about Bruce. The number of times we'd been together was uncountable and I hadn't picked up on the fact that he was gay in all the years I had known him. What was more was that I hadn't twigged that my Cyndi was bi-sexual either. I heard the front door open and close a minute later and guessed that it was Vera leaving and Cyndi came into the lounge and got herself a drink and sat down wanting to know why I was home so early. I told her and then went on to mundane things without Vera being mentioned again.

IT WAS a few days later that Bruce called round, me not knowing that Cyndi had invited him. It was early evening when he rang the doorbell and I answered it.

'Hi, John,' was his greeting, holding up a six pack of beer.

'Hello, Bruce. Come in, anyone with beer is welcome,' I said and he entered and went straight on into the lounge with me following him.

'Hello, Cyndi,' he said, moving over and giving her a kiss on the cheek. 'I haven't come empty handed.'

'I can see that,' she said, taking the cans of beer from his hand and putting them on the coffee table and pulling the wrapper off, got a can out and popped it open. 'Just what the doctor ordered,' she said after taking a mouthful. Both Bruce and myself popped a can each and drank some as we sat down. 'How about a DVD,' she said getting up and moving over to the television set and selected one from beneath the set and inserted into the player and turned both on before sitting back down.

It was a porn movie that she'd put on and it was of two men meeting in a room, kissing before stripping off and showing that they both had an erect cock as they kissed again, stroking each other's erection. She had turned down the sound as we saw one man go down onto his knees to start sucking on the other man's erect cock, taking quite a bit of the length into his mouth. Quite a few close-up shots of the head sliding in and out of the open mouth and getting tongued at the same time.

'That's what I like to see,' Cyndi said. 'Two men sucking on each other. Why don't you suck on Bruce,' she asked, looking at me.

'What?' I replied, shocked at having her make that suggestion.

If you enjoyed this sample then look for **Homos Ubique.**

Also by this Author

About the Author

George Eliot was a famous writer, though at the time, only male authors were recognised. It was in fact the pen name of Mary Ann Evans, a female.

When I started writing, I thought that if a woman could use a male name, why, with me being male, why couldn't I use the name of a female? Though to be different, I made my writer's name from an anagram of my real name.

I wasn't the brightest spark in my school days and it was only while being in the Merchant Navy did I self-educate myself. That being mostly literature, classical music and artists, like Tolstoy, Chopin and Rembrandt. After leaving the navy, I had several jobs, finishing up by being a working boss using my own maxim that 'Management is the art of delegation.'

It's when I became self-employed that I began to write, though sadly, not many of my books can be published because of certain laws that forbid certain aspects of life. This never fazed me for I was really writing just to please myself having a wide range of the human psych.

Having written ninety stories, my only aim now is to reach one hundred. I give thanks to the publishers for at least putting some of my efforts out for others to enjoy as much as I did in the writing of them.

From the Author

Check my page on Amazon and my blog for Updates and interesting info.

Author Central – http://www.amazon.com/Amy-Redek/e/B00A48NQ72
Author Blog – http://amy-redek.awesomeauthors.org/

If you enjoyed any of my books then please share the love and click like on my books in Amazon.

If you write me a review and send me an email I will send you a free book, or many.
(Just know that these emails are filtered by my publisher.)

Good news is always welcome.

One Last Thing, For Kindle Readers...

When you turn the page, Kindle will give you the opportunity to rate this book and share your thoughts on Facebook and Twitter. If you enjoyed my writings, would you please take a few seconds to let your friends know about it? Because... when they enjoy they will be grateful to you and so will I.

Thank You!

Amy Redek
amy_redek@awesomeauthors.org

www.ingramcontent.com/pod-product-compliance
Lightning Source LLC
Chambersburg PA
CBHW071354130626
46556CB00005B/2187